REGINALD

REGINALD

BY

SAKI

(H. H. MUNRO)

GYAN

Published by

Gyan Publishing House
5, Ansari Road
Daryaganj, New Delhi-110002
Phone: 011-47034999, 9811692060
E-mail: books@gyanbooks.com

Distribution Network
gyanbooks.com
India, USA, Canada, UK, Australia, France

ISBN: 978-81-212-7751-8 (PB)
First Published, 1904

2nd Impression 2023

Printed at: Gyan Press, Delhi.

REGINALD
Author: SAKI (H. H. MUNRO)

REGINALD

REGINALD

BY

SAKI

(H. H. MUNRO)

METHUEN & CO.

36 ESSEX STREET W.C.

LONDON

First published, 1904

CONTENTS

	PAGE
Reginald	1
Reginald on Christmas Presents	11
Reginald on the Academy	17
Reginald at the Theatre	25
Reginald's Peace Poem	33
Reginald's Choir Treat	39
Reginald on Worries	47
Reginald on House-Parties	53
Reginald at the Carlton	61
Reginald on Besetting Sins	71
Reginald's Drama	79
Reginald on Tariffs	87
Reginald's Christmas Revel	95
Reginald's Rubaiyat	103
The Innocence of Reginald	111

These sketches originally appeared in the "Westminster Gazette," to the courtesy of the Proprietor of which the author is indebted for permission to republish them.

REGINALD

REGINALD

REGINALD

I DID it—I who should have known better. I persuaded Reginald to go to the McKillops' garden-party against his will.

We all make mistakes occasionally.

"They know you're here, and they'll think it so funny if you don't go. And I want particularly to be in with Mrs. McKillop just now."

"I know, you want one of her smoke Persian kittens as a prospective wife for Wumples—or a husband, is it?" (Reginald has a magnificent scorn for details, other than sartorial.) "And I am expected to undergo social martyrdom to suit the connubial exigencies"—

"Reginald! It's nothing of the kind, only I'm sure Mrs. McKillop would be pleased if I brought you. Young men of your brilliant attractions are rather at a premium at her garden-parties."

"Should be at a premium in heaven," remarked Reginald complacently.

"There will be very few of you there, if that is what you mean. But seriously, there won't be any great strain upon your powers of endurance; I promise you that you shan't have to play croquet, or talk to the Archdeacon's wife, or do anything that is likely to bring on physical prostration. You can just wear your sweetest clothes and a moderately amiable expression, and eat chocolate-creams with the appetite of a *blasé* parrot. Nothing more is demanded of you."

Reginald shut his eyes. "There will be the exhaustingly up-to-date young women who will ask me if I have seen *San Toy*; a less progressive grade who will yearn to hear about the Diamond Jubilee—the historic event, not the horse. With a little encouragement, they will inquire if I saw the Allies march into Paris. Why are women so fond of raking up the past? They're as bad as tailors, who invariably remember what you owe them for a suit long after you've ceased to wear it."

"I'll order lunch for one o'clock; that will give you two and a half hours to dress in."

Reginald puckered his brow into a tortured frown, and I knew that my point was gained. He was debating what tie would go with which waistcoat.

Even then I had my misgivings.

. . . .

During the drive to the McKillops' Reginald was possessed with a great peace, which was not wholly to be accounted for by the fact that he had inveigled his feet into shoes a size too small for them. I misgave more than ever, and having once launched Reginald on to the McKillops' lawn, I established him near a seductive dish of *marrons glacés*, and as far from the Archdeacon's wife as possible; as I drifted away to a diplomatic distance I heard with painful distinctness the eldest Mawkby girl asking him if he had seen *San Toy*.

It must have been ten minutes later, not more, and I had been having *quite* an enjoyable chat with my hostess, and had promised to lend her *The Eternal City* and my recipe for rabbit mayonnaise, and was just about to offer a kind home for her third Persian kitten, when I perceived, out of the corner of my eye, that Reginald was not where I had left him, and that the *marrons glacés* were untasted. At the same moment I became aware that old Colonel Mendoza was essaying to tell his classic story of how he introduced golf into India, and that Reginald was in dangerous proximity. There are occasions when Reginald is caviare to the Colonel.

"When I was at Poona in '76"—

"My dear Colonel," purred Reginald, "fancy admitting such a thing! Such a give-away for one's age! I wouldn't admit being on this planet in '76." (Reginald in his wildest lapses into veracity never admits to being more than twenty-two.)

The Colonel went to the colour of a fig that has attained great ripeness, and Reginald, ignoring my efforts to intercept him, glided away to another part of the lawn. I found him a few minutes later happily engaged in teaching the youngest Rampage boy the approved theory of mixing absinthe, within full earshot of his mother. Mrs. Rampage occupies a prominent place in local Temperance movements.

As soon as I had broken up this unpromising *tête-à-tête* and settled Reginald where he could watch the croquet players losing their tempers, I wandered off to find my hostess and renew the kitten negotiations at the point where they had been interrupted. I did not succeed in running her down at once, and eventually it was Mrs. McKillop who sought me out, and her conversation was not of kittens.

"Your cousin is discussing *Zaza* with the Archdeacon's wife; at least, he is discussing, she is ordering her carriage."

She spoke in the dry, staccato tone of one who repeats a French exercise, and I knew that as far as Millie McKillop was concerned, Wumples was devoted to a lifelong celibacy.

"If you don't mind," I said hurriedly, "I think we'd like our carriage ordered too," and I made a forced march in the direction of the croquet-ground.

I found everyone talking nervously and feverishly of the weather and the war in South Africa, except Reginald, who was reclining in a comfortable chair with the dreamy, far-away look that a volcano might wear just after it had desolated entire villages. The Archdeacon's wife was buttoning up her gloves with a concentrated deliberation that was fearful to behold. I shall have to treble my subscription to her Cheerful Sunday Evenings Fund before I dare set foot in her house again.

At that particular moment the croquet players finished their game, which had been going on without a symptom of finality during the whole afternoon. Why, I ask, should it have stopped precisely when a counter-attraction was so necessary? Everyone seemed to drift towards the area of disturbance, of which the chairs of the Archdeacon's wife and Reginald formed the storm-centre. Conversation flagged, and there settled upon the company that expectant hush that precedes the dawn—when your neighbours don't happen to keep poultry.

"What did the Caspian Sea?" asked Reginald, with appalling suddenness.

There were symptoms of a stampede. The Archdeacon's wife looked at me. Kipling or someone has described somewhere the look a foundered camel gives when the caravan moves on and leaves it to its fate. The peptonised reproach in the good lady's eyes brought the passage vividly to my mind.

I played my last card.

"Reginald, it's getting late, and a sea-mist is coming on." I knew that the elaborate curl over his right eyebrow was not guaranteed to survive a sea-mist.

. . . . .

"Never, never again, will I take you to a garden-party. Never. . . . You behaved abominably. . . . What did the Caspian see?"

A shade of genuine regret for misused opportunities passed over Reginald's face.

"After all," he said, "I believe an apricot tie would have gone better with the lilac waistcoat."

REGINALD ON CHRISTMAS PRESENTS

REGINALD ON CHRISTMAS PRESENTS

I WISH it to be distinctly understood (said Reginald) that I don't want a "George, Prince of Wales" Prayer-book as a Christmas present. The fact cannot be too widely known.

There ought (he continued) to be technical education classes on the science of present-giving. No one seems to have the faintest notion of what anyone else wants, and the prevalent ideas on the subject are not creditable to a civilised community.

There is, for instance, the female relative in the country who "knows a tie is always useful," and sends you some spotted horror that you could only wear in secret or in Tottenham Court Road. It *might* have been useful had she kept it to tie up currant bushes with, when it would have served the double purpose of supporting the branches and frightening away the birds—for it is an admitted fact that the ordinary tomtit of commerce has a sounder æsthetic taste than the average female relative in the country.

Then there are aunts. They are always a difficult class to deal with in the matter of presents. The trouble is that one never catches them really young enough. By the time one has educated them to an appreciation of the fact that one does not wear red woollen mittens in the West End, they die, or quarrel with the family, or do something equally inconsiderate. That is why the supply of trained aunts is always so precarious.

There is my Aunt Agatha, *par exemple*, who sent me a pair of gloves last Christmas, and even got so far as to choose a kind that was being worn and had the correct number of buttons. But—*they were nines!* I sent them to a boy whom I hated intimately: he didn't wear them, of course, but he could have—that was where the bitterness of death came in. It was nearly as consoling as sending white flowers to his funeral. Of course I wrote and told my aunt that they were the one thing that had been wanting to make existence blossom like a rose; I am afraid she thought me frivolous—she comes from the North, where they live in the fear of Heaven and the Earl of Durham. (Reginald affects an exhaustive knowledge of things political, which furnishes an excellent excuse for not discussing them.) Aunts with a dash of foreign extraction in them are the most satisfactory in the way of understanding these things; but if you can't choose your aunt, it is wisest in the long-run to choose the present and send her the bill.

Even friends of one's own set, who might be expected to know better, have curious delusions on the subject. I am *not* collecting copies of the cheaper editions of Omar Khayyam. I gave the last four that I received to the lift-boy, and I like to think of him reading them, with FitzGerald's notes, to his aged mother. Lift-boys always have aged mothers; shows such nice feeling on their part, I think.

Personally, I can't see where the difficulty in choosing suitable presents lies. No boy who had brought himself up properly could fail to appreciate one of those decorative bottles of liqueurs that are so reverently staged in Morel's window—and it wouldn't in the least matter if one did get duplicates. And there would always be the supreme moment of dreadful uncertainty whether it was *crême de menthe* or Chartreuse—like the expectant thrill on seeing your partner's hand turned up at bridge. People may say what they like about the decay of Christianity; the religious system that produced green Chartreuse can never really die.

And then, of course, there are liqueur glasses, and crystallised fruits, and tapestry curtains, and heaps of other necessaries of life that make really sensible presents—not to speak of luxuries, such as having one's bills paid, or getting something quite sweet in the way of jewellery. Unlike the alleged Good Woman of the Bible, I'm not above rubies. When found, by the way, she must have been rather a problem at Christmas-time; nothing short of a blank cheque would have fitted the situation. Perhaps it's as well that she's died out.

The great charm about me (concluded Reginald) is that I am so easily pleased. But I draw the line at a "Prince of Wales" Prayer-book.

REGINALD ON THE ACADEMY

REGINALD ON THE ACADEMY

"ONE goes to the Academy in self-defence," said Reginald. "It is the one topic one has in common with the Country Cousins."

"It is almost a religious observance with them," said the Other. "A kind of artistic Mecca, and when the good ones die they go"—

"To the Chantrey Bequest. The mystery is *what* they find to talk about in the country."

"There are two subjects of conversation in the country: Servants, and Can fowls be made to pay? The first, I believe, is compulsory, the second optional."

"As a function," resumed Reginald, "the Academy is a failure."

"You think it would be tolerable without the pictures?"

"The pictures are all right, in their way;

after all, one can always *look* at them if one is bored with one's surroundings, or wants to avoid an imminent acquaintance."

"Even that doesn't always save one. There is the inevitable female whom you met once in Devonshire, or the Matoppo Hills, or somewhere, who charges up to you with the remark that it's funny how one always meets people one knows at the Academy. Personally, I *don't* think it funny."

"I suffered in that way just now," said Reginald plaintively, "from a woman whose word I had to take that she had met me last summer in Brittany."

"I hope you were not too brutal?"

"I merely told her with engaging simplicity that the art of life was the avoidance of the unattainable."

"Did she try and work it out on the back of her catalogue?"

"Not there and then. She murmured something about being 'so clever.' Fancy coming to the Academy to be clever!"

"To be clever in the afternoon argues that one is dining nowhere in the evening."

"Which reminds me that I can't remember whether I accepted an invitation from you to dine at Kettner's to-night."

"On the other hand, I can remember with startling distinctness not having asked you to."

"So much certainty is unbecoming in the young; so we'll consider that settled. What were you talking about? Oh, pictures. Personally, I rather like them; they are so refreshingly real and probable, they take one away from the unrealities of life."

"One likes to escape from oneself occasionally."

"That is the disadvantage of a portrait; as a rule, one's bitterest friends can find nothing more to ask than the faithful unlikeness that goes down to posterity as oneself. I hate posterity—it's so fond of having the last word. Of course, as regards portraits, there are exceptions."

"For instance?"

"To die before being painted by Sargent is to go to heaven prematurely."

"With the necessary care and impatience, you may avoid that catastrophe."

"If you're going to be rude," said Reginald, "I shall dine with you to-morrow night as well. The chief vice of the Academy," he continued, "is its nomenclature. Why, for instance, should an obvious trout-stream with a palpable rabbit sitting in the foreground be called 'an evening dream of unbeclouded peace,' or something of that sort?"

"You think," said the Other, "that a name should economise description rather than stimulate imagination?"

"Properly chosen, it should do both. There is my lady kitten at home, for instance; I've called it Derry."

"Suggests nothing to my imagination but protracted sieges and religious animosities. Of course, I don't know your kitten"—

"Oh, you're silly. It's a sweet name, and it answers to it—when it wants to. Then, if there are any unseemly noises in the night, they can be explained succinctly: Derry and Toms."

"You might almost charge for the advertisement. But as applied to pictures, don't you think your system would be too subtle, say, for the Country Cousins?"

"Every reformation must have its victims. You can't expect the fatted calf to share the enthusiasm of the angels over the prodigal's return. Another darling weakness of the Academy is that none of its luminaries must 'arrive' in a hurry. You can see them coming for years, like a Balkan trouble or a street improvement, and by the time they have painted a thousand or so square yards of canvas, their work begins to be recognised."

"Someone who Must Not be Contradicted said that a man must be a success by the time he's thirty, or never."

"To have reached thirty," said Reginald, "is to have failed in life."

REGINALD AT THE THEATRE

REGINALD AT THE THEATRE

"AFTER all," said the Duchess vaguely, "there are certain things you can't get away from. Right and wrong, good conduct and moral rectitude, have certain well-defined limits."

"So, for the matter of that," replied Reginald, "has the Russian Empire. The trouble is that the limits are not always in the same place."

Reginald and the Duchess regarded each other with mutual distrust, tempered by a scientific interest. Reginald considered that the Duchess had much to learn; in particular, not to hurry out of the Carlton as though afraid of losing one's last 'bus. A woman, he said, who is careless of disappearances is capable of leaving town before Goodwood, and dying at the wrong moment of an unfashionable disease.

The Duchess thought that Reginald did not exceed the ethical standard which circumstances demanded.

"Of course," she resumed combatively, "it's the prevailing fashion to believe in perpetual change and mutability, and all that sort of thing, and to say we are all merely an improved form of primeval ape — of course you subscribe to that doctrine?"

"I think it decidedly premature; in most people I know the process is far from complete."

"And equally of course you are quite irreligious?"

"Oh, by no means. The fashion just now is a Roman Catholic frame of mind with an Agnostic conscience: you get the mediæval picturesqueness of the one with the modern conveniences of the other."

The Duchess suppressed a sniff. She was one of those people who regard the Church of England with patronising affection, as if it were something that had grown up in their kitchen garden.

"But there are other things," she continued, "which I suppose are to a certain extent sacred even to you. Patriotism, for instance, and Empire, and Imperial responsibility, and blood-is-thicker-than-water, and all that sort of thing."

Reginald waited for a couple of minutes

before replying, while the Lord of Rimini temporarily monopolised the acoustic possibilities of the theatre.

"That is the worst of a tragedy," he observed, "one can't always hear oneself talk. Of course I accept the Imperial idea and the responsibility. After all, I would just as soon think in Continents as anywhere else. And some day, when the season is over and we have the time, you shall explain to me the exact blood-brotherhood and all that sort of thing that exists between a French Canadian and a mild Hindoo and a Yorkshireman, for instance."

"Oh, well, 'dominion over palm and pine,' you know," quoted the Duchess hopefully; "of course we mustn't forget that we're all part of the great Anglo-Saxon Empire."

"Which for its part is rapidly becoming a suburb of Jerusalem. A very pleasant suburb, I admit, and quite a charming Jerusalem. But still a suburb."

"Really, to be told one's living in a suburb when one is conscious of spreading the benefits of civilisation all over the world! Philanthropy—I suppose you will say *that* is a comfortable delusion; and yet even you must admit that whenever want or misery or starvation is known to exist, however distant or difficult of access, we instantly organise relief on the most generous scale, and distribute it, if need be, to the uttermost ends of the earth."

The Duchess paused, with a sense of ultimate triumph. She had made the same observation at a drawing-room meeting, and it had been extremely well received.

"I wonder," said Reginald, "if you have ever walked down the Embankment on a winter night?"

"Gracious, no, child! Why do you ask?"

"I didn't; I only wondered. And even your philanthropy, practised in a world where everything is based on competition, must have a debit as well as a credit account. The young ravens cry for food."

"And are fed."

"Exactly. Which presupposes that something else is fed upon."

"Oh, you're simply exasperating. You've been reading Nietzsche till you haven't got any sense of moral proportion left. May I ask if you are governed by *any* laws of conduct whatever?"

"There are certain fixed rules that one observes for one's own comfort. For instance, never be flippantly rude to any inoffensive, grey-bearded stranger that you may meet in pine forests or hotel smoking-rooms on the Continent. It always turns out to be the King of Sweden."

"The restraint must be dreadfully irksome to you. When I was younger, boys of your age used to be nice and innocent."

"Now we are only nice. One must specialise in these days. Which reminds me of the man I read of in some sacred book who was given a choice of what he most desired. And because he didn't ask for titles and honours and dignities, but only for immense wealth, these other things came to him also."

"I am sure you didn't read about him in any sacred book."

"Yes; I fancy you will find him in Debrett."

REGINALD'S PEACE POEM

REGINALD'S PEACE POEM

"I'M writing a poem on Peace," said Reginald, emerging from a sweeping operation through a tin of mixed biscuits, in whose depths a macaroon or two might yet be lurking.

"Something of the kind seems to have been attempted already," said the Other.

"Oh, I know; but I may never have the chance again. Besides, I've got a new fountain pen. I don't pretend to have gone on any very original lines; in writing about Peace the thing is to say what everybody else is saying, only to say it better. It begins with the usual ornithological emotion—

'When the widgeon westward winging
Heard the folk Vereeniginging,
Heard the shouting and the singing'"—

"Vereeniginging is good, but why widgeon?"

"Why not? Anything that winged westward would naturally begin with a *w*."

"Need it wing westward?"

"The bird must go somewhere. You wouldn't have it hang around and look foolish. Then I've brought in something about the heedless hartebeest galloping over the deserted veldt."

"Of course you know it's practically extinct in those regions?"

"I can't help *that*, it gallops so nicely. I make it have all sorts of unexpected yearnings—

'Mother, may I go and maffick,
Tear around and hinder traffic?'

Of course you'll say there would be no traffic worth bothering about on the bare and sun-scorched veldt, but there's no other word that rhymes with maffick."

"Seraphic?"

Reginald considered. "It might do, but I've got a lot about angels later on. You must have angels in a Peace poem; I know dreadfully little about their habits."

"They can do unexpected things, like the hartebeest."

"Of course. Then I turn on London,

the City of Dreadful Nocturnes, resonant with hymns of joy and thanksgiving—

'And the sleeper, eye unlidding,
Heard a voice for ever bidding
Much farewell to Dolly Gray;
Turning weary on his truckle-
Bed he heard the honey-suckle
Lauded in apiarian lay.'

Longfellow at his best wrote nothing like that."

"I agree with you."

"I wish you wouldn't. I've a sweet temper, but I can't stand being agreed with. And I'm so worried about the aasvogel."

Reginald stared dismally at the biscuit-tin, which now presented an unattractive array of rejected cracknels.

"I believe," he murmured, "if I could find a woman with an unsatisfied craving for cracknels, I should marry her."

"What is the tragedy of the aasvogel?" asked the Other sympathetically.

"Oh, simply that there's no rhyme for it. I thought about it all the time I was dressing — it's dreadfully bad for one to think whilst one's dressing—and all lunch-time, and I'm still hung up over it. I feel like those unfortunate automobilists who achieve an unenviable motoriety by coming to a hopeless stop with their cars in the most crowded thoroughfares. I'm afraid I shall have to drop the aasvogel, and it did give such lovely local colour to the thing."

"Still you've got the heedless hartebeest."

"And quite a decorative bit of moral admonition—when you've worried the meaning out—

'Cease, War, thy bubbling madness that the wine shares,
And bid thy legions turn their swords to mine shares.'

Mine shares seems to fit the case better than ploughshares. There's lots more about the blessings of Peace, shall I go on reading it?"

"If I must make a choice, I think I would rather they went on with the war."

REGINALD'S CHOIR TREAT

REGINALD'S CHOIR TREAT

"NEVER," wrote Reginald to his most darling friend, "be a pioneer. It's the Early Christian that gets the fattest lion."

Reginald, in his way, was a pioneer.

None of the rest of his family had anything approaching Titian hair or a sense of humour, and they used primroses as a table decoration.

It follows that they never understood Reginald, who came down late to breakfast, and nibbled toast, and said disrespectful things about the universe. The family ate porridge, and believed in everything, even the weather forecast.

Therefore the family was relieved when the vicar's daughter undertook the reformation of Reginald. Her name was Amabel; it was the vicar's one extravagance. Amabel was accounted a beauty and intellectually gifted; she never played tennis, and was reputed to have read Maeterlinck's *Life of the Bee*. If you abstain from tennis *and* read Maeterlinck in a small country village, you are of necessity intellectual. Also she had been twice to Fécamp to pick up a good French accent from the Americans staying there; consequently she had a knowledge of the world which might be considered useful in dealings with a worldling.

Hence the congratulations in the family when Amabel undertook the reformation of its wayward member.

Amabel commenced operations by asking her unsuspecting pupil to tea in the vicarage garden; she believed in the healthy influence of natural surroundings, never having been in Sicily, where things are different.

And like every woman who has ever preached repentance to unregenerate youth, she dwelt on the sin of an empty life, which always seems so much more scandalous in the country, where people rise early to see if a new strawberry has happened during the night.

Reginald recalled the lilies of the field, "which simply sat and looked beautiful, and defied competition."

"But that is not an example for us to follow," gasped Amabel.

"Unfortunately, we can't afford to. You don't know what a world of trouble I take in trying to rival the lilies in their artistic simplicity."

"You are really indecently vain of your appearance. A good life is infinitely preferable to good looks."

"You agree with me that the two are incompatible. I always say beauty is only sin deep."

Amabel began to realise that the battle is not always to the strong-minded. With the immemorial resource of her sex, she abandoned the frontal attack, and laid stress on her unassisted labours in parish work, her mental loneliness, her discouragements—and at the right moment she produced strawberries and cream. Reginald was obviously affected by the latter, and when his preceptress suggested that he might begin the strenuous life by helping her to supervise the annual outing of the bucolic infants who composed the local choir, his eyes shone with the dangerous enthusiasm of a convert.

Reginald entered on the strenuous life

alone, as far as Amabel was concerned. The most virtuous women are not proof against damp grass, and Amabel kept her bed with a cold. Reginald called it a dispensation; it had been the dream of his life to stage-manage a choir outing. With strategic insight, he led his shy, bullet-headed charges to the nearest woodland stream and allowed them to bathe; then he seated himself on their discarded garments and discoursed on their immediate future, which, he decreed, was to embrace a Bacchanalian procession through the village. Forethought had provided the occasion with a supply of tin whistles, but the introduction of a he-goat from a neighbouring orchard was a brilliant afterthought. Properly, Reginald explained, there should have been an outfit of panther skins; as it was, those who had spotted handkerchiefs were allowed to wear them, which they did with thankfulness. Reginald recognised the impossibility, in the time at his disposal, of teaching his shivering neophytes a chant in honour of Bacchus, so he started them off with a more familiar, if less appropriate, temperance hymn. After all, he said, it is the spirit of the thing that counts. Following the etiquette of dramatic authors on first nights, he remained discreetly in the background while the procession, with extreme diffidence and the goat, wound its way lugubriously towards the village. The singing had died down long before the main street was reached, but the miserable wailing of pipes brought the inhabitants to their doors. Reginald said he had seen something like it in pictures; the villagers had seen nothing like it in their lives, and remarked as much freely.

Reginald's family never forgave him. They had no sense of humour.

REGINALD ON WORRIES

REGINALD ON WORRIES

I HAVE (said Reginald) an aunt who worries. She's not really an aunt—a sort of amateur one, and they aren't really worries. She is a social success, and has no domestic tragedies worth speaking of, so she adopts any decorative sorrows that are going, myself included. In that way she's the antithesis, or whatever you call it, to those sweet, uncomplaining women one knows who have seen trouble, and worn blinkers ever since. Of course, one just loves them for it, but I must confess they make me uncomfy; they remind one so of a duck that goes flapping about with forced cheerfulness long after its head's been cut off. Ducks have *no* repose. Now, my aunt has a shade of hair that suits her, and a cook who quarrels with the other servants, which is always a hopeful sign, and a conscience that's absentee for about eleven months of the year, and only turns up at Lent to annoy her husband's people, who are considerably Lower than the angels, so to speak: with all these natural advantages—she says her particular tint of bronze is a natural advantage, and there can be no two opinions as to the advantage—of course she has to send out for her afflictions, like those restaurants where they haven't got a licence. The system has this advantage, that you can fit your unhappinesses in with your other engagements, whereas real worries have a way of arriving at meal-times, and when you're dressing, or other solemn moments. I knew a canary once that had been trying for months and years to hatch out a family, and everyone looked upon it as a blameless infatuation, like the sale of Delagoa Bay, which would be an annual loss to the Press agencies if it ever came to pass; and one day the bird really did bring it off, in the middle of family prayers. I say the middle, but it was also the end: you can't go on being thankful for daily bread when you are wondering what on earth very new canaries expect to be fed on.

At present she's rather in a Balkan state of mind about the treatment of the Jews in Roumania. Personally, I think the Jews have estimable qualities; they're so kind to their poor—and to our rich. I daresay in Roumania the cost of living beyond one's income isn't so great. Over here the trouble is that so many people who have money to throw about seem to have such vague ideas where to throw it. That fund, for instance, to relieve the victims of sudden disasters—what is a sudden disaster? There's Marion Mulciber, who *would* think she could play bridge, just as she would think she could ride down a hill on a bicycle; on that occasion she went to a hospital, now she's gone into a Sisterhood—lost all she had, you know, and gave the rest to Heaven. Still, you can't call it a sudden calamity; *that* occurred when poor dear Marion was born. The doctors said at the time that she couldn't live more than a fortnight, and she's been trying ever since to see if she could. Women are so opinionated.

And then there's the Education Question—not that I can see that there's anything to worry about in that direction. To my mind, education is an absurdly over-rated affair. At least, one never took it very seriously at school, where everything was done to bring it prominently under one's notice. Anything that is worth knowing one practically teaches oneself, and the rest obtrudes itself sooner or later. The reason one's elders know so comparatively little is because they have to unlearn so much that they acquired by way of education before we were born. Of course I'm a believer in Nature-study; as I said to Lady Beauwhistle, if you want a lesson in elaborate artificiality, just watch the studied unconcern of a Persian cat entering a crowded salon, and then go and practise it for a fortnight. The Beauwhistles weren't born in the Purple, you know, but they're getting there on the instalment system—so much down, and the rest when you feel like it. They have kind hearts, and they never forget birthdays. I forget what he was, something in the City, where the patriotism comes from; and she—oh, well, her frocks are built in Paris, but she wears them with a strong English accent. So public-spirited of her. I think she must have been very strictly brought up, she's so desperately anxious to do the wrong thing correctly. Not that it really matters nowadays, as I told her: I know some perfectly virtuous people who are received everywhere.

REGINALD ON HOUSE-PARTIES

REGINALD ON HOUSE-PARTIES

THE drawback is, one never really *knows* one's hosts and hostesses. One gets to know their fox-terriers and their chrysanthemums, and whether the story about the go-cart can be turned loose in the drawing-room, or must be told privately to each member of the party, for fear of shocking public opinion; but one's host and hostess are a sort of human hinterland that one never has the time to explore.

There was a fellow I stayed with once in Warwickshire who farmed his own land, but was otherwise quite steady. Should never have suspected him of having a soul, yet not very long afterwards he eloped with a lion-tamer's widow and set up as a golf-instructor somewhere on the Persian Gulf; dreadfully immoral, of course, because he was only an indifferent player, but still, it showed imagination. His wife was really to be pitied, because he had been the only person in the house who understood how to manage the cook's temper, and now she has to put "D.V." on her dinner invitations. Still, that's better than a domestic scandal; a woman who leaves her cook never wholly recovers her position in Society.

I suppose the same thing holds good with the hosts; they seldom have more than a superficial acquaintance with their guests, and so often just when they do get to know you a bit better, they leave off knowing you altogether. There was *rather* a breath of winter in the air when I left those Dorsetshire people. You see, they had asked me down to shoot, and I'm not particularly immense at that sort of thing. There's such a deadly sameness about partridges; when you've missed one, you've missed the lot—at least, that's been my experience. And they tried to rag me in the smoking-room about not being able to hit a bird at five yards, a sort of bovine ragging that suggested cows buzzing round a gadfly and thinking they were teasing it. So I got up the next morning at early dawn—I know it was dawn, because there were lark-noises in the sky, and the grass looked as if it had been left out all night—and hunted up the most conspicuous thing in the bird line that I could find, and measured the distance, as nearly as it would let me, and shot away all I knew. They said afterwards that it was a tame bird; that's simply *silly*, because it was awfully wild at the first few shots. Afterwards it quieted down a bit, and when its legs had stopped waving farewells to the landscape I got a gardener-boy to drag it into the hall, where everybody must see it on their way to the breakfast-room. I breakfasted upstairs myself. I gathered afterwards that the meal was tinged with a very unchristian spirit. I suppose it's unlucky to bring peacock's feathers into a house; anyway, there was a blue-pencilly look in my hostess's eye when I took my departure.

Some hostesses, of course, will forgive anything, even unto pavonicide (is there such a word?), as long as one is nice-looking and sufficiently unusual to counterbalance some of the others; and there *are* others—the girl, for instance, who reads Meredith, and appears at meals with unnatural punctuality in a frock that's made at home and repented at leisure. She eventually finds her way to India and gets married, and comes home to admire the Royal Academy, and to imagine that an indifferent prawn curry is for ever an effective substitute for all that we have been taught to believe is luncheon. It's then that she is really dangerous; but at her worst she is never quite so bad as the woman who fires *Exchange and Mart* questions at you without the least provocation. Imagine the other day, just when I was doing my best to understand half the things I was saying, being asked by one of those seekers after country home truths how many fowls she could keep in a run ten feet by six, or whatever it was! I told her whole crowds, as long as she kept the door shut, and the idea didn't seem to have struck her before; at least, she brooded over it for the rest of dinner.

Of course, as I say, one never really *knows* one's ground, and one may make mistakes occasionally. But then one's mistakes sometimes turn out assets in the long-run: if we had never bungled away our American colonies we might never have had the boy from the States to teach us how to wear our hair and cut our clothes, and we must get our ideas from somewhere, I suppose. Even the Hooligan was probably invented in China centuries before we thought of him. England must wake up, as the Duke of Devonshire said the other day; wasn't it? Oh, well, it was someone else. Not that I ever indulge in despair about the Future; there always have been men who have gone about despairing of the Future, and when the Future arrives it says nice, superior things about their having acted according to their lights. It is dreadful to think that other people's grandchildren may one day rise up and call one amiable.

There are moments when one sympathises with Herod.

REGINALD AT THE CARLTON

REGINALD AT THE CARLTON

"A MOST variable climate," said the Duchess; "and how unfortunate that we should have had that very cold weather at a time when coal was so dear! So distressing for the poor."

"Someone has observed that Providence is always on the side of the big dividends," remarked Reginald.

The Duchess ate an anchovy in a shocked manner; she was sufficiently old-fashioned to dislike irreverence towards dividends.

Reginald had left the selection of a feeding-ground to her womanly intuition, but he chose the wine himself, knowing that womanly intuition stops short at claret. A woman will cheerfully choose husbands for her less attractive friends, or take sides in a political controversy without the least knowledge of the issues involved—but no woman ever cheerfully chose a claret.

"Hors d'œuvres have always a pathetic

interest for me," said Reginald: "they remind me of one's childhood that one goes through, wondering what the next course is going to be like—and during the rest of the menu one wishes one had eaten more of the hors d'œuvres. Don't you love watching the different ways people have of entering a restaurant? There is the woman who races in as though her whole scheme of life were held together by a one-pin despotism which might abdicate its functions at any moment; it's really a relief to see her reach her chair in safety. Then there are the people who troop in with an-unpleasant-duty-to-perform air, as if they were angels of Death entering a plague city. You see that type of Briton very much in hotels abroad. And nowadays there are always the Johannesbourgeois, who bring a Cape-to-Cairo atmosphere with them — what may be called the Rand Manner, I suppose."

"Talking about hotels abroad," said the Duchess, "I am preparing notes for a lecture at the Club on the educational effects of modern travel, dealing chiefly with the moral side of the question. I was talking to Lady Beauwhistle's aunt the other day

—she's just come back from Paris, you know. Such a sweet woman"—

"And so silly. In these days of the over-education of women she's quite refreshing. They say some people went through the siege of Paris without knowing that France and Germany were at war; but the Beauwhistle aunt is credited with having passed the whole winter in Paris under the impression that the Humberts were a kind of bicycle. . . . Isn't there a bishop or somebody who believes we shall meet all the animals we have known on earth in another world? How frightfully embarrassing to meet a whole shoal of whitebait you had last known at Prince's! I'm sure in my nervousness I should talk of nothing but lemons. Still, I daresay they would be quite as offended if one hadn't eaten them. I know if I were served up at a cannibal feast I should be dreadfully annoyed if anyone found fault with me for not being tender enough, or having been kept too long."

"My idea about the lecture," resumed the Duchess hurriedly, "is to inquire whether promiscuous Continental travel doesn't tend to weaken the moral fibre of the social conscience. There are people one knows, quite nice people when they are in England, who are so *different* when they are anywhere the other side of the Channel."

"The people with what I call Tauchnitz morals," observed Reginald. "On the whole, I think they get the best of two very desirable worlds. And, after all, they charge so much for excess luggage on some of those foreign lines that it's really an economy to leave one's reputation behind one occasionally."

"A scandal, my dear Reginald, is as much to be avoided at Monaco or any of those places as at Exeter, let us say."

"Scandal, my dear Irene—I may call you Irene, mayn't I?"

"I don't know that you have known me long enough for that."

"I've known you longer than your godparents had when they took the liberty of calling you that name. Scandal is merely the compassionate allowance which the gay make to the humdrum. Think how many blameless lives are brightened by the blazing indiscretions of other people. Tell me, who is the woman with the old lace at the table on our left? Oh, *that* doesn't matter; it's quite the thing nowadays to stare at people as if they were yearlings at Tattersall's."

"Mrs. Spelvexit? Quite a charming woman; separated from her husband"—

"Incompatibility of income?"

"Oh, nothing of that sort. By miles of frozen ocean, I was going to say. He explores ice-floes and studies the movements of herrings, and has written a most interesting book on the home-life of the Esquimaux; but naturally he has very little home-life of his own."

"A husband who comes home with the Gulf Stream *would* be rather a tied-up asset."

"His wife is exceedingly sensible about it. She collects postage-stamps. Such a resource. Those people with her are the Whimples, very old acquaintances of mine; they're always having trouble, poor things."

"Trouble is not one of those fancies you can take up and drop at any moment; it's like a grouse-moor or the opium-habit—once you start it you've got to keep it up."

"Their eldest son was such a disappointment to them; they wanted him to be a linguist, and spent no end of money on having him taught to speak—oh, dozens of languages!—and then he became a Trappist monk. And the youngest, who was intended for the American marriage market, has developed political tendencies, and writes pamphlets about the housing of the poor. Of course it's a most important question, and I devote a good deal of time to it myself in the mornings; but, as Laura Whimple says, it's as well to have an establishment of one's own before agitating about other people's. She feels it very keenly, but she always maintains a cheerful appetite, which I think is so unselfish of her."

"There are different ways of taking disappointment. There was a girl I knew who nursed a wealthy uncle through a long illness, borne by her with Christian fortitude, and then he died and left his money to a swine-fever hospital. She found she'd about cleared stock in fortitude by that time, and now she gives drawing-room recitations. That's what I call being vindictive."

"Life is full of its disappointments," observed the Duchess, "and I suppose the art of being happy is to disguise them as illusions. But that, my dear Reginald, becomes more difficult as one grows older."

"I think it's more generally practised than you imagine. The young have aspirations that never come to pass, the old have reminiscences of what never happened. It's only the middle-aged who are really conscious of their limitations—that is why one should be so patient with them. But one never is."

"After all," said the Duchess, "the disillusions of life may depend on our way of assessing it. In the minds of those who come after us we may be remembered for qualities and successes which we quite left out of the reckoning."

"It's not always safe to depend on the commemorative tendencies of those who come after us. There may have been disillusionments in the lives of the mediæval saints, but they would scarcely have been better pleased if they could have foreseen that their names would be associated nowadays chiefly with racehorses and the cheaper clarets. And now, if you can tear yourself away from the salted almonds, we'll go and have coffee under the palms that are so necessary for our discomfort."

REGINALD ON BESETTING SINS

REGINALD ON BESETTING SINS

THE WOMAN WHO TOLD THE TRUTH

THERE was once (said Reginald) a woman who told the truth. Not all at once, of course, but the habit grew upon her gradually, like lichen on an apparently healthy tree. She had no children—otherwise it might have been different. It began with little things, for no particular reason except that her life was a rather empty one, and it is so easy to slip into the habit of telling the truth in little matters. And then it became difficult to draw the line at more important things, until at last she took to telling the truth about her age; she said she was forty-two and five months—by that time, you see, she was veracious even to months. It may have been pleasing to the angels, but her elder sister was not gratified. On the Woman's birthday, instead of the opera-tickets which she had hoped for, her sister gave her a view of Jerusalem from the Mount of Olives, which is not quite the same thing. The revenge of an elder sister may be long in coming, but, like a South-Eastern express, it arrives in its own good time.

The friends of the Woman tried to dissuade her from over-indulgence in the practice, but she said she was wedded to the truth; whereupon it was remarked that it was scarcely logical to be so much together in public. (No really provident woman lunches regularly with her husband if she wishes to burst upon him as a revelation at dinner. He must have time to forget; an afternoon is not enough.) And after a while her friends began to thin out in patches. Her passion for the truth was not compatible with a large visiting-list. For instance, she told Miriam Klopstock *exactly* how she looked at the Ilexes' ball. Certainly Miriam had asked for her candid opinion, but the Woman prayed in church every Sunday for peace in our time, and it was not consistent.

It was unfortunate, everyone agreed, that she had no family; with a child or two in the house, there is an unconscious check upon too free an indulgence in the truth. Children are given us to discourage our better emotions. That is why the stage, with all its efforts, can never be as artificial as life; even in an Ibsen drama one must reveal to the audience things that one would suppress before the children or servants.

Fate may have ordained the truth-telling from the commencement and should justly bear some of the blame; but in having no children the Woman was guilty, at least, of contributory negligence.

Little by little she felt she was becoming a slave to what had once been merely an idle propensity; and one day she knew. Every woman tells ninety per cent. of the truth to her dressmaker; the other ten per cent. is the irreducible minimum of deception beyond which no self-respecting client trespasses. Madame Draga's establishment was a meeting-ground for naked truths and overdressed fictions, and it was here, the Woman felt, that she might make a final effort to recall the artless mendacity of past days. Madame herself was in an inspiring mood, with the air of a sphinx who knew all things and preferred to forget most of them. As a War Minister she might have been celebrated, but she was content to be merely rich.

"If I take it in here, and—Miss Howard, one moment, if you please—and there, and round like this—so—I really think you will find it quite easy."

The Woman hesitated; it seemed to require such a small effort to simply acquiesce in Madame's views. But habit had become too strong. "I'm afraid," she faltered, "it's just the least little bit in the world too"—

And by that least little bit she measured the deeps and eternities of her thraldom to fact. Madame was not best pleased at being contradicted on a professional matter, and when Madame lost her temper you usually found it afterwards in the bill.

And at last the dreadful thing came, as the Woman had foreseen all along that it must; it was one of those paltry little truths with which she harried her waking hours. On a raw Wednesday morning, in a few ill-chosen words, she told the cook that she drank. She remembered the scene afterwards as vividly as though it had been painted in her mind by Abbey. The cook was a good cook, as cooks go; and as cooks go she went.

Miriam Klopstock came to lunch the next day. Women and elephants never forget an injury.

REGINALD'S DRAMA

REGINALD'S DRAMA

REGINALD closed his eyes with the elaborate weariness of one who has rather nice eyelashes and thinks it useless to conceal the fact.

"One of these days," he said, "I shall write a really great drama. No one will understand the drift of it, but everyone will go back to their homes with a vague feeling of dissatisfaction with their lives and surroundings. Then they will put up new wall-papers and forget."

"But how about those that have oak panelling all over the house?" said the Other.

"They can always put down new stair-carpets," pursued Reginald, "and, anyhow, I'm not responsible for the audience having a happy ending. The play would be quite sufficient strain on one's energies. I should get a bishop to say it was immoral and beautiful—no dramatist has thought of that before, and everyone would come to condemn the bishop, and they would stay on out of sheer nervousness. After all, it requires a great deal of moral courage to leave in a marked manner in the middle of the second act, when your carriage isn't ordered till twelve. And it would commence with wolves worrying something on a lonely waste—you wouldn't see them, of course; but you would hear them snarling and scrunching, and I should arrange to have a wolfy fragrance suggested across the footlights. It would look so well on the programmes, 'Wolves in the first act, by Jamrach.' And old Lady Whortleberry, who never misses a first night, would scream. She's always been nervous since she lost her first husband. He died quite abruptly while watching a county cricket match; two and a half inches of rain had fallen for seven runs, and it was supposed that the excitement killed him. Anyhow, it gave her quite a shock; it was the first husband she'd lost, you know, and now she always screams if anything thrilling happens too soon after dinner. And after the audience had heard the Whortleberry scream the thing would be fairly launched."

"And the plot?"

"The plot," said Reginald, "would be

one of those little everyday tragedies that one sees going on all round one. In my mind's eye there is the case of the Mudge-Jervises, which in an unpretentious way has quite an Enoch Arden intensity underlying it. They'd only been married some eighteen months or so, and circumstances had prevented their seeing much of each other. With him there was always a foursome or something that had to be played and replayed in different parts of the country, and she went in for slumming quite as seriously as if it was a sport. With her, I suppose, it was. She belonged to the Guild of the Poor Dear Souls, and they hold the record for having nearly reformed a washerwoman. No one has ever really reformed a washerwoman, and that is why the competition is so keen. You can rescue charwomen by fifties with a little tea and personal magnetism, but with washerwomen it's different; wages are too high. This particular laundress, who came from Bermondsey or some such place, was really rather a hopeful venture, and they thought at last that she might be safely put in the window as a specimen of successful work. So they had her paraded at a drawing-room "At Home" at Agatha Camelford's; it was sheer bad luck that some liqueur chocolates had been turned loose by mistake among the refreshments—really liqueur chocolates, with very little chocolate. And of course the old soul found them out, and cornered the entire stock. It was like finding a whelk-stall in a desert, as she afterwards partially expressed herself. When the liqueurs began to take effect, she started to give them imitations of farmyard animals as they know them in Bermondsey. She began with a dancing bear, and you know Agatha doesn't approve of dancing, except at Buckingham Palace under proper supervision. And then she got up on the piano and gave them an organ monkey; I gather she went in for realism rather than a Maeterlinckian treatment of the subject. Finally, she fell into the piano and said she was a parrot in a cage, and for an impromptu performance I believe she was very word-perfect; no one had heard anything like it, except Baroness Boobelstein, who has attended sittings of the Austrian Reichsrath. Agatha is trying the Rest-cure at Buxton."

"But the tragedy?"

"Oh, the Mudge-Jervises. Well, they were getting along quite happily, and their married life was one continuous exchange of picture-postcards; and then one day they were thrown together on some neutral ground where foursomes and washerwomen overlapped, and discovered that they were hopelessly divided on the Fiscal Question. They have thought it best to separate, and she is to have the custody of the Persian kittens for nine months in the year—they go back to him for the winter, when she is abroad. There you have the material for a tragedy drawn straight from life—and the piece could be called 'The Price They Paid for Empire.' And of course one would have to work in studies of the struggle of hereditary tendency against environment and all that sort of thing. The woman's father could have been an Envoy to some of the smaller German Courts; that's where she'd get her passion for visiting the poor, in spite of the most careful upbringing. *C'est le premier pa qui compte*, as the cuckoo said when it swallowed its foster-parent. That, I think, is quite clever."

"And the wolves?"

"Oh, the wolves would be a sort of elusive undercurrent in the background that would never be satisfactorily explained. After all, life teems with things that have no earthly reason. And whenever the characters could think of nothing brilliant to say about marriage or the War Office, they could open a window and listen to the howling of the wolves. But that would be very seldom."

REGINALD ON TARIFFS

REGINALD ON TARIFFS

I'M not going to discuss the Fiscal Question (said Reginald); I wish to be original. At the same time, I think one suffers more than one realises from the system of free imports. I should like, for instance, a really prohibitive duty put upon the partner who declares on a weak red suit and hopes for the best. Even a free outlet for compressed verbiage doesn't balance matters. And I think there should be a sort of bounty-fed export (is that the right expression?) of the people who impress on you that you ought to take life seriously. There are only two classes that really can't help taking life seriously—schoolgirls of thirteen and Hohenzollerns; they might be exempt. Albanians come under another heading; they take life whenever they get the opportunity. The one Albanian that I was ever on speaking terms with was rather a decadent example. He was a Christian and a grocer, and I don't fancy he had ever killed anybody. I didn't like to question him on the subject—that showed my delicacy. Mrs. Nicorax says I have no delicacy; she hasn't forgiven me about the mice. You see, when I was staying down there, a mouse used to cake-walk about my room half the night, and none of their silly patent traps seemed to take its fancy as a bijou residence, so I determined to appeal to the better side of it—which with mice is the inside. So I called it Percy, and put little delicacies down near its hole every night, and that kept it quiet while I read Max Nordau's *Degeneration* and other reproving literature, and went to sleep. And now she says there is a whole colony of mice in that room.

That isn't where the indelicacy comes in. She went out riding with me, which was entirely her own suggestion, and as we were coming home through some meadows she made a quite unnecessary attempt to see if her pony would jump a rather messy sort of brook that was there. It wouldn't. It went with her as far as the water's edge, and from that point Mrs. Nicorax went on alone. Of course I had to fish her out from the bank, and my riding-breeches are not cut with a view to salmon-fishing—it's rather an art even to ride in them. Her habit-skirt was one of those open questions that need not be adhered to in emergencies, and on this occasion it remained behind in some water-weeds. She wanted me to fish about for that too, but I felt I had done enough Pharaoh's daughter business for an October afternoon, and I was beginning to want my tea. So I bundled her up on to her pony, and gave her a lead towards home as fast as I cared to go. What with the wet and the unusual responsibility, her abridged costume did not stand the pace particularly well, and she got quite querulous when I shouted back that I had no pins with me—and no string. Some women expect so much from a fellow. When we got into the drive she wanted to go up the back way to the stables, but the ponies *know* they always get sugar at the front door, and I never attempt to hold a pulling pony; as for Mrs. Nicorax, it took her all she knew to keep a firm hand on her seceding garments, which, as her maid remarked afterwards, were more *tout* than *ensemble.* Of course nearly the whole house-party were out on the lawn watching the sunset—the only day this month that it's occurred to the sun to show itself, as Mrs. Nic. viciously observed—and I shall never forget the expression on her husband's face as we pulled up. "My darling, this is too much!" was his first spoken comment; taking into consideration the state of her toilet, it was the most brilliant thing I had ever heard him say, and I went into the library to be alone and scream. Mrs. Nicorax says I have no delicacy.

Talking about tariffs, the lift-boy, who reads extensively between the landings, says it won't do to tax raw commodities. What, exactly, is a raw commodity? Mrs. Van Challaby says men are raw commodities till you marry them; after they've struck Mrs. Van C., I can fancy they pretty soon become a finished article. Certainly she's had a good deal of experience to support her opinion. She lost one husband in a railway accident, and mislaid another in the Divorce Court, and the current one has just got himself squeezed in a Beef Trust. "What was he doing in a Beef Trust, anyway?" she asked tearfully, and I suggested that perhaps he had an unhappy home. I only said it for the sake of making conversation; which it did. Mrs. Van Challaby said things about me which in her calmer moments she would have hesitated to spell. It's a pity people can't discuss fiscal matters without getting wild. However, she wrote next day to ask if I could get her a Yorkshire terrier of the size and shade that's being worn now, and that's as near as a woman can be expected to get to owning herself in the wrong. And she will tie a salmon-pink bow to its collar, and call it " Reggie," and take it with her everywhere—like poor Miriam Klopstock, who *would* take her Chow with her to the bathroom, and while she was bathing it was playing at she-bears with her garments. Miriam is always late for breakfast, and she wasn't really missed till the middle of lunch.

However, I'm not going any further into the Fiscal Question. Only I should like to be protected from the partner with a weak red tendency.

REGINALD'S CHRISTMAS REVEL

REGINALD'S CHRISTMAS REVEL

THEY say (said Reginald) that there's nothing sadder than victory except defeat. If you've ever stayed with dull people during what is alleged to be the festive season, you can probably revise that saying. I shall never forget putting in a Christmas at the Babwolds'. Mrs. Babwold is some relation of my father's—a sort of to-be-left-till-called-for cousin — and that was considered sufficient reason for my having to accept her invitation at about the sixth time of asking; though why the sins of the father should be visited by the children—you won't find any notepaper in that drawer; that's where I keep old menus and first-night programmes.

Mrs. Babwold wears a rather solemn personality, and has never been known to smile, even when saying disagreeable things to her friends or making out the Stores list.

She takes her pleasures sadly. A state elephant at a Durbar gives one a very similar impression. Her husband gardens in all weathers. When a man goes out in the pouring rain to brush caterpillars off rose-trees, I generally imagine his life indoors leaves something to be desired; anyway, it must be very unsettling for the caterpillars.

Of course there were other people there. There was a Major Somebody who had shot things in Lapland, or somewhere of that sort; I forget what they were, but it wasn't for want of reminding. We had them cold with every meal almost, and he was continually giving us details of what they measured from tip to tip, as though he thought we were going to make them warm under-things for the winter. I used to listen to him with a rapt attention that I thought rather suited me, and then one day I quite modestly gave the dimensions of an okapi I had shot in the Lincolnshire fens. The Major turned a beautiful Tyrian scarlet (I remember thinking at the time that I should like my bathroom hung in that colour), and I think that at that moment he almost found it in his heart to dislike me. Mrs. Babwold put on a first-aid-to-the-injured expression, and asked him why he didn't publish a book of his sporting reminiscences; it would be *so* interesting. She didn't remember till afterwards that he had given her two fat volumes on the subject, with his portrait and autograph as a frontispiece and an appendix on the habits of the Arctic mussel.

It was in the evening that we cast aside the cares and distractions of the day and really lived. Cards were thought to be too frivolous and empty a way of passing the time, so most of them played what they called a book game. You went out into the hall—to get an inspiration, I suppose—then you came in again with a muffler tied round your neck and looked silly, and the others were supposed to guess that you were "Wee MacGreegor." I held out against the inanity as long as I decently could, but at last, in a lapse of good-nature, I consented to masquerade as a book, only I warned them that it would take some time to carry out. They waited for the best part of forty minutes, while I went and played wineglass skittles with the page-boy in the pantry; you play it with a champagne cork, you know, and the one who knocks down the most glasses without breaking them wins. I won, with four unbroken out of seven; I think William suffered from over-anxiousness. They were rather mad in the drawing-room at my not having come back, and they weren't a bit pacified when I told them afterwards that I was "At the end of the passage."

"I never did like Kipling," was Mrs. Babwold's comment, when the situation dawned upon her. "I couldn't see anything clever in *Earthworms out of Tuscany*—or is that by Darwin?"

Of course these games are very educational, but, personally, I prefer bridge.

On Christmas evening we were supposed to be specially festive in the Old English fashion. The hall was horribly draughty, but it seemed to be the proper place to revel in, and it was decorated with Japanese fans and Chinese lanterns, which gave it a very Old English effect. A young lady with a confidential voice favoured us with a long recitation about a little girl who died or did something equally hackneyed, and then the Major gave us a graphic account of a struggle he had with a wounded bear. I privately wished that the bears would win sometimes on these occasions; at least they wouldn't go vapouring about it afterwards. Before we had time to recover our spirits, we were indulged with some thought-reading by a young man whom one knew instinctively had a good mother and an indifferent tailor —the sort of young man who talks unflaggingly through the thickest soup, and smooths his hair dubiously as though he thought it might hit back. The thought-reading was rather a success; he announced that the hostess was thinking about poetry, and she admitted that her mind was dwelling on one of Austin's odes. Which was near enough. I fancy she had been really wondering whether a scrag-end of mutton and some cold plum-pudding would do for the kitchen dinner next day. As a crowning dissipation, they all sat down to play progressive halma, with milk-chocolate for prizes. I've been carefully brought up, and I don't like to play games of skill for milk-chocolate, so I invented a headache and retired from the scene. I had been preceded a few minutes earlier by Miss Langshan-Smith, a rather formidable lady, who always got up at some uncomfortable hour in the morning, and gave you the impression that she had been in communication with most of the European Governments before breakfast.

There was a paper pinned on her door with a signed request that she might be called particularly early on the morrow. Such an opportunity does not come twice in a lifetime. I covered up everything except the signature with another notice, to the effect that before these words should meet the eye she would have ended a misspent life, was sorry for the trouble she was giving, and would like a military funeral. A few minutes later I violently exploded an air-filled paper bag on the landing, and gave a stage moan that could have been heard in the cellars. Then I pursued my original intention and went to bed. The noise those people made in forcing open the good lady's door was positively indecorous; she resisted gallantly, but I believe they searched her for bullets for about a quarter of an hour, as if she had been a historic battlefield.

I hate travelling on Boxing Day, but one must occasionally do things that one dislikes.

REGINALD'S RUBAIYAT

REGINALD'S RUBAIYAT

THE other day (confided Reginald), when I was killing time in the bathroom and making bad resolutions for the New Year, it occurred to me that I would like to be a poet. The chief qualification, I understand, is that you must be born. Well, I hunted up my birth certificate, and found that I was all right on that score, and then I got to work on a Hymn to the New Year, which struck me as having possibilities. It suggested extremely unusual things to absolutely unlikely people, which I believe is the art of first-class catering in any department. Quite the best verse in it went something like this—

> "Have you heard the groan of a gravelled grouse,
> Or the snarl of a snaffled snail
> (Husband or mother, like me, or spouse),
> Have you lain a-creep in the darkened house
> Where the wounded wombats wail?"

It was quite improbable that anyone

had, you know, and that's where it stimulated the imagination and took people out of their narrow, humdrum selves. No one has ever called me narrow or humdrum, but even I felt worked up now and then at the thought of that house with the stricken wombats in it. It simply wasn't nice. But the editors were unanimous in leaving it alone; they said the thing had been done before and done worse, and that the market for that sort of work was extremely limited.

It was just on the top of that discouragement that the Duchess wanted me to write something in her album—something Persian, you know, and just a little bit decadent—and I thought a quatrain on an unwholesome egg would meet the requirements of the case. So I started in with—

> "Cackle, cackle, little hen,
> How I wonder if and when
> Once you laid the egg that I
> Met, alas! too late. Amen."

The Duchess objected to the Amen, which I thought gave an air of forgiveness and *chose jugée* to the whole thing; also she said it wasn't Persian enough, as though I were trying to sell her a kitten whose mother had married for love rather than pedigree. So I recast it entirely, and the new version read—

> "The hen that laid thee moons ago, who knows
> In what Dead Yesterday her shades repose;
> To some election turn thy waning span
> And rain thy rottenness on fiscal foes."

I thought there was enough suggestion of decay in that to satisfy a jackal, and to me there was something infinitely pathetic and appealing in the idea of the egg having a sort of St. Luke's summer of commercial usefulness. But the Duchess begged me to leave out any political allusions; she's the president of a Women's Something or other, and she said it might be taken as an endorsement of deplorable methods. I never can remember which Party Irene discourages with her support, but I shan't forget an occasion when I was staying at her place and she gave me a pamphlet to leave at the house of a doubtful voter, and some grapes and things for a woman who was suffering from a chill on the top of a patent medicine. I thought it much cleverer to give the grapes to the former and the political literature to the sick woman, and the Duchess was quite absurdly annoyed about it afterwards. It seems the leaflet was addressed "To those about to wobble"—I wasn't responsible for the silly title of the thing—and the woman never recovered; anyway, the voter was completely won over by the grapes and jellies, and I think that should have balanced matters. The Duchess called it bribery, and said it might have compromised the candidate she was supporting; he was expected to subscribe to church funds and chapel funds, and football and cricket clubs and regattas, and bazaars and beanfeasts and bellringers, and poultry shows and ploughing matches, and reading-rooms and choir outings, and shooting trophies and testimonials, and anything of that sort; but bribery would not have been tolerated.

I fancy I have perhaps more talent for electioneering than for poetry, and I was really getting extended over this quatrain business. The egg began to be unmanageable, and the Duchess suggested something with a French literary ring about it. I hunted back in my mind for the most familiar French classic that I could take liberties with, and after a little exercise of memory I turned out the following:—

> "Hast thou the pen that once the gardener had?
> I have it not; and know, these pears are bad.
> Oh, larger than the horses of the Prince
> Are those the general drives in Kaikobad."

Even that didn't altogether satisfy Irene; I fancy the geography of it puzzled her. She probably thought Kaikobad was an unfashionable German spa, where you'd meet matrimonial bargain-hunters and emergency Servian kings. My temper was beginning to slip its moorings by that time I look rather nice when I lose my temper. (I hoped you would say I lose it very often. I mustn't monopolise the conversation.)

"Of course, if you want something really Persian and passionate, with red wine and bulbuls in it," I went on to suggest; but she grabbed the book away from me.

"Not for worlds. Nothing with red wine or passion in it. Dear Agatha gave me the album, and she would be mortified to the quick"—

I said I didn't believe Agatha had a quick, and we got quite heated in arguing the matter. Finally, the Duchess declared I shouldn't write anything nasty in her book, and I said I wouldn't write anything in her nasty book, so there wasn't a very wide point of difference between us. For the rest of the afternoon I pretended to be sulking, but I was really working back to that quatrain, like a fox-terrier that's buried a deferred lunch in a private flower-bed. When I got an opportunity I hunted up Agatha's autograph, which had the front page all to itself, and, copying her prim handwriting as well as I could, I inserted above it the following Thibetan fragment:—

"With Thee, oh, my Beloved, to do a dâk
(a dâk I believe is a sort of uncomfortable post-journey)
On the pack-saddle of a grunting yak,
With never room for chilling chaperone,
'Twere better than a Panhard in the Park."

That Agatha would get on to a yak in company with a lover even in the comparative seclusion of Thibet is unthinkable. I very much doubt if she'd do it with her own husband in the privacy of the Simplon tunnel. But poetry, as I've remarked before, should always stimulate the imagination.

By the way, when you asked me the other day to dine with you on the 14th, I said I was dining with the Duchess. Well, I'm not. I'm dining with you.

THE INNOCENCE OF REGINALD

THE INNOCENCE OF REGINALD

REGINALD slid a carnation of the newest shade into the buttonhole of his latest lounge coat, and surveyed the result with approval. "I am just in the mood," he observed, "to have my portrait painted by someone with an unmistakable future. So comforting to go down to posterity as 'Youth with a Pink Carnation' in catalogue-company with 'Child with Bunch of Primroses,' and all that crowd."

"Youth," said the Other, "should suggest innocence."

"But never act on the suggestion. I don't believe the two ever really go together. People talk vaguely about the innocence of a little child, but they take mighty good care not to let it out of their sight for twenty minutes. The watched pot never boils over. I knew a boy once who really was innocent; his parents were in Society, but they never gave him a moment's anxiety from his infancy. He believed in company prospectuses, and in the purity of elections, and in women marrying for love, and even in a system for winning at roulette. He never quite lost his faith in it, but he dropped more money than his employers could afford to lose. When last I heard of him, he was believing in his innocence; the jury weren't. All the same, I really am innocent just now of something everyone accuses me of having done, and so far as I can see, their accusations will remain unfounded."

"Rather an unexpected attitude for you."

"I love people who do unexpected things. Didn't you always adore the man who slew a lion in a pit on a snowy day? But about this unfortunate innocence. Well, quite long ago, when I'd been quarrelling with more people than usual, you among the number—it must have been in November, I never quarrel with you too near Christmas—I had an idea that I'd like to write a book. It was to be a book of personal reminiscences, and was to leave out nothing."

"Reginald!"

"Exactly what the Duchess said when

I mentioned it to her. I was provoking and said nothing, and the next thing, of course, was that everyone heard that I'd written the book and got it in the press. After that, I might have been a gold-fish in a glass bowl for all the privacy I got. People attacked me about it in the most unexpected places, and implored or commanded me to leave out things that I'd forgotten had ever happened. I sat behind Miriam Klopstock one night in the dress circle at His Majesty's, and she began at once about the incident of the Chow dog in the bathroom, which she insisted must be struck out. We had to argue it in a disjointed fashion, because some of the people wanted to listen to the play, and Miriam takes nines in voices. They had to stop her playing in the 'Macaws' Hockey Club because you could hear what she thought when her shins got mixed up in a scrimmage for half a mile on a still day. They are called the Macaws because of their blue-and-yellow costumes, but I understand there was nothing yellow about Miriam's language. I agreed to make one alteration, as I pretended I had got it a Spitz instead of a Chow, but beyond that

I was firm. She megaphoned back two minutes later, 'You promised you would never mention it; don't you ever keep a promise?' When people had stopped glaring in our direction, I replied that I'd as soon think of keeping white mice. I saw her tearing little bits out of her programme for a minute or two, and then she leaned back and snorted, 'You're not the boy I took you for,' as though she were an eagle arriving at Olympus with the wrong Ganymede. That was her last audible remark, but she went on tearing up her programme and scattering the pieces around her, till one of her neighbours asked with immense dignity whether she should send for a wastepaper basket. I didn't stay for the last act.

"Then there is Mrs.—oh, I never can remember her name; she lives in a street that the cabmen have never heard of, and is at home on Wednesdays. She frightened me horribly once at a private view by saying mysteriously, 'I oughtn't to be here, you know; this is one of my days.' I thought she meant that she was subject to periodical outbreaks and was expecting an attack at any moment. So embarrassing if she had suddenly taken it into her head that she was Cesar Borgia or St. Elizabeth of Hungary. That sort of thing would make one unpleasantly conspicuous even at a private view. However, she merely meant to say that it was Wednesday, which at the moment was incontrovertible. Well, she's on quite a different tack to the Klopstock. She doesn't visit anywhere very extensively, and, of course, she's awfully keen for me to drag in an incident that occurred at one of the Beauwhistle garden-parties, when she says she accidentally hit the shins of a Serene Somebody or other with a croquet mallet and that he swore at her in German. As a matter of fact, he went on discoursing on the Gordon-Bennett affair in French. (I never can remember if it's a new submarine or a divorce. Of course, how stupid of me!) To be disagreeably exact, I fancy she missed him by about two inches — over-anxiousness, probably—but she likes to think she hit him. I've felt that way with a partridge which I always imagine keeps on flying strong, out of false pride, till it's the other side of the hedge. She said she could tell me everything she was wearing on the occasion. I said I didn't want my book to read like a laundry list, but she explained that she didn't mean those sort of things.

"And there's the Chilworth boy, who can be charming as long as he's content to be stupid and wear what he's told to; but he gets the idea now and then that he'd like to be epigrammatic, and the result is like watching a rook trying to build a nest in a gale. Since he got wind of the book, he's been persecuting me to work in something of his about the Russians and the Yalu Peril, and is quite sulky because I won't do it.

"Altogether, I think it would be rather a brilliant inspiration if you were to suggest a fortnight in Paris."

Printed by Morrison & Gibb Limited, *Edinburgh.*

Reginald

Saki (H. H. Munro)

In this collection, we delve into Reginald's world, where he offers his witty commentary on a wide array of subjects, including Christmas presents, the Academy, theater, and house parties. Reginald's unique perspectives on life come to the forefront as he shares his thoughts on peace, worries, and personal weaknesses. From critiquing dramas to pondering tariffs and the holiday season, Reginald's distinctive charm and humor are ever-present. His adventures span from Russia to encounters with Lady Anne's reserved nature, lost items, peculiar shopping habits, and even a Turkish calamity. These stories invite readers on a delightful journey into the amusing and mischievous realm of Reginald, filled with clever and unexpected twists.

Hector Hugh Munro (1870–1916), widely recognized by his pen name Saki, and also frequently referred to as H. H. Munro, was a British writer renowned for his sharp, mischievous, and at times darkly humorous stories that serve as satirical commentary on Edwardian society and its culture. Renowned for his mastery of the short story format, he is often likened to literary figures like O. Henry and Dorothy Parker. Saki drew inspiration from the works of Oscar Wilde, Lewis Carroll, and Rudyard Kipling, and in turn, left an indelible influence on writers such as A. A. Milne, Noël Coward, and P. G. Wodehouse.

Price: ₹ 250

ISBN: 978-81-212-7751-8

9 788121 277518

GYAN PUBLISHING HOUSE

email- books@gyanbooks.com

Distribution Network:

www.gyanbooks.com

India, USA, Canada, UK, Australia & France

साहित्य निबंधावली

राहुल सांकृत्यायन